DEAN

Stories first published 1993 by Buzz Books
an imprint of Reed Children's Books
Michelin House, 81 Fulham Road, London SW3 6RB
and Auckland, Melbourne, Singapore and Toronto
This edition published 1994 by Dean
in association with Methuen Children's Books

ISBN 0 603 55246 3
Printed in China

Contents

Rupert and the Silent Flute

It was a wintry Friday afternoon. After school, Rupert, Bill, Algy and Gregory set off for Rupert's house. Mrs Bear had invited them all for tea.

When they reached Nutwood Common, Algy ran across the grass, then turned round and threw his tennis ball high into the air.

"Catch, Rupert!" he shouted.

Rupert darted forward and the tennis ball dropped neatly into his cupped hands.

"To me, Rupert!" called Gregory.

Rupert threw the ball gently to Gregory.

It was an easy catch, but as Gregory reached out, he slipped on a patch of mud. The ball whistled past his ear and fell onto a gorse bush at the edge of the woods.

Gregory jumped to his feet and skipped over to the bush where the ball had landed.

"I can get it back if I use a stick," he said, and he bent down to look under the bush. "Here's one!"

Rupert, Bill and Algy watched Gregory use the little stick to free the tennis ball. Then, to their surprise, Gregory put the stick to his lips.

"Look!" he cried. "It's got holes in it, like a flute!" And he blew into the hollow stick.

But nothing happened.

He tried again, blowing harder this time, but still not a peep came out of the little flute.

"Never mind," said Rupert. "Let's go and see what's for tea!"

As they walked, Gregory marched in front, pretending to play his new flute.

"Left, right! Left, right!" he chanted.

Algy decided to play a joke on Gregory.

"Left turn!" he shouted.

Gregory turned smartly to his left and stomped up the path to Nutwood Police Station. All the way he played his wooden flute, but still no sound came from it.

"Halt!" barked a deep voice. "About turn! Quick march!"

In the doorway of the Police Station stood Constable Growler. Gregory hurried back

down the path to join his friends. Together they set off again for Rupert's house.

Mrs Bear was waiting at the cottage.

"I'm sorry we're late," Rupert told his mother as they laid the table for tea. "But Gregory slipped on some mud and — "

He looked round the room. Bill and Algy were sitting at the table, but there was no sign of Gregory.

"Look, Rupert," laughed Mrs Bear, pointing out of the window.

There was Gregory, marching up and down the garden path, still playing his silent flute!

After tea, Rupert waved goodbye to his friends and went back inside the cottage. It was a wintry evening, and his father was putting some more wood on the fire.

"What a funny little log," said Mr Bear, picking up a stick to throw into the grate.

"Oh, no! That's not a log!" cried Rupert. "It's Gregory's flute!"

"Here," said Mr Bear, handing Rupert the flute. "You can take it round to Gregory tomorrow."

Early the next morning, Rupert heard someone talking to his father.

"...all the way up the path to the Police Station!" said a deep, stern voice.

It was Constable Growler! Rupert hoped that Gregory wasn't in trouble for marching up and down outside the Police Station.

"Constable Growler said that some of his spring flowers have bloomed already!" said Mr Bear after the policeman had gone.

"But it's far too soon!" said Mrs Bear.
Rupert pointed out of the kitchen window.
"Look, Daddy!" he cried. "Your flowers are out, too!"
"How peculiar," said Mr Bear, shaking his head. "It's as if they think that spring is here already."
After breakfast, Rupert set off for Gregory's house with the flute. He soon came to Nutwood Police Station, where he found the Wise Old Goat carefully inspecting Constable Growler's flowers.
"Hello," said Rupert. "What brings you to Nutwood?"
"Constable Growler rang this morning," replied his friend. "He's very puzzled about his flowers. And so, I must admit, am I!"
"The flowers in my father's garden are blooming, too," said Rupert. He held out the hollow stick in his hand. "Look at this flute we found yesterday."

Rupert told his friend all about Gregory's little flute. He showed the Wise Old Goat how Gregory had marched up and down outside the Police Station blowing the flute.
His friend chuckled, and then looked serious.
"Oh, dear," said the Wise Old Goat. "May I hear the flute again?"
Rupert blew into the silent flute once more, and the Wise Old Goat listened very carefully.
"You cannot hear a sound," said the Wise Old Goat. "But to the Imps of Spring, it is as clear as a bell! This flute is their special signal to wake the flowers from their winter sleep. Only they can hear the music and only the King of the Imps may play the flute."
"The King must have left it under the bush where Gregory found it," said Rupert.
The Wise Old Goat nodded.

"And when Gregory tried to play the flute, the Imps followed the sound," he said. "They set Constable Growler's flowers blooming, and your father's, before it was time."

"Look!" cried Rupert. "Here comes Gregory!"

"Hello, Rupert," said Gregory. "I was just on my way to your house to get my flute."

Before Rupert could say anything, the door to the Police Station opened.

"Good morning, all," said Constable Growler. "Now, Gregory Guineapig, I want a word with you! I hear that you like playing the whistle?"

"Oh, dear," said Rupert.

The village policeman took something out of his jacket pocket. "Well, try this!" he said, handing Gregory a shiny tin police whistle.

Gregory put the whistle in his mouth. Suddenly, the air was filled with a piercing sound. Rupert, the Wise Old Goat — even Constable Growler — covered their ears as

"Please tell him that Gregory didn't mean any harm. He was only playing," said Rupert.
"Even the King of the Imps was young once," laughed the Wise Old Goat as he strode off towards Nutwood Common. He looked back at Gregory. "But maybe not that young!"

Gregory blew with all his might.
"I must hurry," shouted the Wise Old Goat above the din. "I shall take the flute back to the King of the Imps at once!"

Rupert
and the Dizzy Donkey

"It's a perfect drying day!" said Mrs Bear to Rupert one morning. "The sun is out and there's a lovely fresh breeze!"

Rupert carried the basket of wet clothes into the garden, and watched as his mother hung them out to dry. The shirts flapped in the wind, as if they were eager to fly away.

"It would be fun to fly a kite on a day like this," said Rupert. "May I ask Willie Mouse if he'd like to take his kite out?"

"Of course you may," said Mrs Bear. She went into the larder and found two shiny red apples. "Here's one for you, and one for Willie, in case you feel hungry later."

Rupert knocked at his friend's front door. Willie peeped timidly through the window.

"Oh, it's you, Rupert," he said, and he opened the door.

"Hello, Willie," said Rupert, "I was just wondering if..."

Willie's whiskers fluttered in the breeze.

"I bet I know what you're going to ask!" he said. "Come in while I put on my shoes. Then we'll take my kite to the top of the hill and see how high it will go!"

Willie Mouse was ready in a moment, and together they set off across the common and up the lane that led to the foot of the hill.

As they climbed the grassy slope, Rupert remembered the two shiny red apples. He had left them on Willie Mouse's kitchen table.

"Hold on tight, Willie!" called Rupert.

The string raced through Willie's fingers as the kite flew higher and higher.

Rupert ran to Willie's side and gripped the string with all his might, but then another fierce gust of wind tugged the string so hard that even Rupert had to let go.

"Look!" cried Rupert, as the kite sailed away. "It's going to catch in that tree!"

Rupert and Willie raced to the tall oak tree which had caught the kite in its branches.

"It's a very tall tree," said Willie, nervously.

At the top of the hill, Willie unrolled the ball of string and ran through the grass with the box kite behind him. Suddenly, a gust of wind caught the kite and tried to pull it away from the little mouse.

"Help!" cried Willie. "If I let go of the string, I'll never see my kite again!"

"Don't worry, Willie," said Rupert, "I'll bring your kite down."

Rupert climbed the oak tree carefully, holding its sturdy branches tightly, until he was level with the kite.

"I can't reach from here," he told Willie.

"I shall have to crawl along this branch."

Willie watched as Rupert edged his way nearer to the kite.

"I've got the kite!" Rupert called down to his friend as he clutched the string. "What a view! I can see everything from up here. There's Nutwood, and there's Popton, and — wait a minute, that's funny — "

"What is it?" asked Willie, but Rupert was

already on his way back down.

He handed Willie his kite and told him what he had seen from the treetop.

"There's a donkey in the farmer's field down the lane," he said, "and it looked as if it was dancing! Since the wind is much too strong for kite flying, shall we go and see what's the matter with the donkey?"

The little bear eagerly led his friend back down the hill.

"Listen," he said. From the other side of the hedge there came an angry bellow.

A few yards further on, they found a stile. Rupert was about to climb over when suddenly he heard the thunder of hooves, and there stood the donkey.

"It doesn't look very friendly," said Willie.

"No, and here's why," replied Rupert. "The poor donkey has an old bag of rubbish caught on his ear. I expect it was left behind by picnickers from the city. Every time he shakes his head, the bag flaps about. No wonder he's feeling dizzy!"

Rupert reached carefully towards the carrier bag.

"I must try to lift it off his ear without hurting him," he told Willie.

But as he leaned over the stile, the donkey took fright and started shaking its head even more anxiously.

"He won't let me near enough to help him," said Rupert. "We must find a way to calm him down." Rupert thought for a moment.

"I know! Willie, will you please run back to Nutwood and ask the Chinese Conjurer if he has any spells for charming angry beasts?"

Rupert waited by the stile as the little mouse skipped down the lane. He hoped that Willie would be back soon.

"Don't worry," he told the donkey. "We'll help you take off that horrible bag. Just wait a little bit longer, please."

It seemed to be a very long wait. Rupert tried to stroke the donkey's back, but every time he reached his hand across the stile, the frightened creature jumped away.

Then, from along the lane, he heard Willie Mouse talking to someone. It must be the Chinese Conjurer!

"Rupert!" called Willie. "The Conjurer was out, but I've brought Tigerlily instead."

"Hello Rupert," said the Conjurer's daughter, "I hear you need some magic!"

"It's this poor donkey," said Rupert. "He must be charmed into lying down so that I

can take that nasty bag off his ear."

"I know just the spell!" said Tigerlily.

Rupert was worried. What if Tigerlily's spell went wrong? Then he had an idea.

"We don't need a spell, Tigerlily," he replied. "Just sing the donkey the sweetest lullaby you know."

Tigerlily understood at once, and began singing quietly. When the donkey heard the beautiful old Chinese melody, it stopped jumping and listened, its head tilted to one side. Slowly, it lay down in the long grass, closed its big brown eyes, and fell asleep.

"Thank you, Tigerlily," said Rupert.

He climbed over the stile and carefully slid the bag's handles off the donkey's ear.

"We must put that in a litter bin where it won't harm any other creatures," he said, passing the bag across the stile to Willie.

"Look out, Rupert!" cried Willie.

Rupert turned round to see the donkey, wide awake again, strolling towards him.

"Hello, Donkey," he said. "That bag won't hurt you any more."

The donkey moved its head up and down, as if it were nodding to Rupert. Then it gently butted him, walked a few steps away, and waited.

"He wants me to follow him!" said Rupert.

"Be careful," warned Willie Mouse.

Willie and Tigerlily watched the donkey lead Rupert through a gap in the hedge and into another field. Then they heard a strange noise. It sounded as if the donkey was butting something rather hard.

"Oh, no! What's happened?" cried Willie.

Rupert walked back through the gap in the hedge. The donkey trotted happily behind him.

"He wants to say thank you," said Rupert.

"But what was that awful sound?" Willie asked his friend.

"Oh, he was just helping the wind to shake the trees in that orchard," replied Rupert, bringing his hands out from behind his back. There, in his open palms, were three ripe, shiny, red apples to munch on the way home to Nutwood.

Rupert
and the Rope Trick

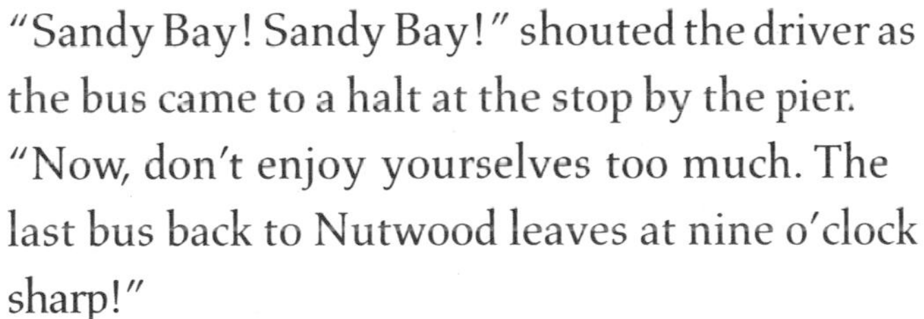

"Sandy Bay! Sandy Bay!" shouted the driver as the bus came to a halt at the stop by the pier. "Now, don't enjoy yourselves too much. The last bus back to Nutwood leaves at nine o'clock sharp!"

Rupert and his mother stepped off the bus, followed by Bill Badger and Algy Pug.

"This way," said Mrs Bear, leading them down the steps to the beach.

Rupert and Bill followed her onto the sand and began to unpack the picnic.

"Where's Algy?" asked Mrs Bear.

Rupert and Bill looked all around, but there was no sign of him.

"I'm up here!" came a voice from the pier. "There's a poster for a magic show tonight. It says that the magician has discovered

an ancient rope trick and... Are those egg sandwiches?"

Algy raced down the steps to join his friends on the picnic rug.

After lunch, Rupert, Bill and Algy cleared all the litter away.

"Do you think that the magician has really found an old rope trick?" asked Algy.

"No," said Bill, "he's probably invented a new one. It will be done with very fine wires and special lights, I expect."

Rupert looked up at the pier. The theatre was at the very end. The waves were crashing against the rocks below the theatre. It would be an exciting place to see a magic show!

"I'm going to walk to the end of the pier," he told his mother.

"That's a good idea," said Mrs Bear. "Do you and Algy want to go, too?" she asked Bill.

"No," said Bill Badger. "We'd rather stay on the beach."

"There's a little cove beyond this one," said Algy. "We're going to explore it!"

Rupert climbed the steps up to the pier, and walked out along it. When he was half-way out, he stopped to look back at the beach. In the distance, he could see Bill and Algy running across the warm sand towards the next bay.

At the entrance to the theatre, there was a poster for that evening's show: Tonight! The Great Magic Show. Doctor Sanders will perform an ancient rope trick which he discovered in the land of the Pharaohs!

A photograph was pinned to the poster, showing a mysterious-looking man wearing a dark cloak. He was holding a coil of rope, like a sleeping snake.

Rupert was fascinated. He decided to ask his mother if they might see the show before catching the bus back to Nutwood.

He was about to run back to the beach when he spotted something right at the end of the pier. It was a telescope.

Rupert put a penny in the slot and looked through the eyepiece.

In the distance, he could see the little cove which Algy and Bill had gone to explore. There they were, pottering happily amongst the rock-pools. Then Rupert had a shock. Through the telescope he saw that the sea had cut off Bill and Algy's path back to Sandy Bay. They were trapped!

Rupert walked back along the pier. He tried to think of a way to rescue his friends before the tide rose too high. Perhaps he could find a local boatman to ferry them back. He began walking faster — and ran straight into a tall man carrying a small leather suitcase.

"Can't you look where you're going?" asked the stranger crossly.

"I'm very sorry," said Rupert, "but I'm in a terrible hurry. My friends have been cut off by the tide!"

"I see," replied the man. "Well, you had better go for help — and quickly!"

Rupert looked at the stranger again, then glanced at the picture on the theatre door.

"You're Doctor Sanders!" he exclaimed. "Won't you use your magic to help my friends? Please?"

"I'm not sure if I can," said the magician, and he frowned thoughtfully. "Wait! I have an idea. Follow me, little bear! We'll take the cliff path."

The man strode off along the pier, with Rupert running behind him.

"I don't understand," began Rupert. "How do you think we can rescue Algy and Bill from the top of the cliff?"

The mysterious magician smiled, and walked ever more quickly towards the clifftop. Rupert followed, trying his best to keep up with the magician's long strides.

"We must make haste," Doctor Sanders told Rupert. "The tide is in a hurry today. See how quickly the water rises!"

Rupert looked down to the bay below. Algy and Bill were on a tiny rock, and the waves were coming closer and closer.

Doctor Sanders put down his suitcase and strode to the edge of the cliff.

"Keep back," he told Rupert, "It's very dangerous to stand near the edge."

Out of the suitcase he took a cloak as dark as

night, and wrapped it around his shoulders. Next, he put on a pair of pure white gloves. Lastly, the magician took out a coil of very old rope.

"The ancient rope trick!" cried Rupert.

"Bill! Algy!" shouted Doctor Sanders down into the bay. "I'm going to throw down a magic rope. Please don't let it fall in the sea!"

Bill and Algy held out their hands as the magician threw the coiled rope down from the clifftop.

"Got it!" shouted Bill.

"Good," said Doctor Sanders. "Carefully now, lay the rope on the sand. Take the end, Bill, and hold on very tightly!"

As Bill gripped the rope, the magician recited an ancient spell. Suddenly, as if it were waking up, the rope began to uncoil. Bill held on tight

as the magic rope rose from the sand, carrying him up and away from the lapping waves.

Rupert watched Doctor Sanders conjure the rope higher and higher, until Bill could step on to the clifftop.

"Well done," said the magician. "Now it's your turn, Algy!" He threw the coiled rope back down towards the bay. Once again, he spoke the strange old words, and while Algy clutched the rope, it rose to the top of the cliff.

"It really is magic!" said Bill, as he watched the mysterious man pack his cloak, gloves and rope back into their suitcase.

"Did you not believe it was?" asked Doctor Sanders. "You must come to my show tonight. Then you will see some more of my real magic!"

He snapped his fingers, and there in his palm were some theatre tickets.

"Three?" he asked.

"May I have one for my mother?" asked Rupert. With a flourish, the magician produced another ticket.

"Thank you, Doctor Sanders," said Rupert.

"And thank you for rescuing us!" cried Algy and Bill.

"A magician must always use his magic wisely," replied Doctor Sanders. Without another word, he turned, and walked briskly away along the cliff path.

That evening, before the bus left for Nutwood, Rupert and Mrs Bear, Algy Pug and Bill Badger went to see the Great Magic Show.

"And now, for my final trick," announced Doctor Sanders, "I will need a volunteer from the audience. Ah, yes, the little bear in the front row!"

Rupert stepped on to the stage and stood timidly in the spotlight. Doctor Sanders turned to him and whispered behind his cloak, "It wouldn't be fair for you to go home without having a go, would it?"

Then he turned to the audience. "Ladies and Gentlemen, may I present Rupert and the mysterious Rope Trick!"

Rupert
and the Vanishing Scarecrow

Dr Chimp walked into the classroom and opened the register.

"We have a new pupil starting this term," he told the class. "Kevin's family has only just moved to Nutwood, and he hasn't met any friends yet."

Doctor Chimp looked round the classroom.

"Would one of you like to show him around the school?" he asked.

At once, the pupils all put up their hands.

"Good," said the teacher. "I can see that Kevin is going to be well looked after. Rupert, I asked Kevin to wait in my office. Please bring him to meet the class."

Rupert was pleased. He walked happily out of the classroom and down the corridor to the

teacher's office. The door was open.
"Kevin!" he called from outside the office.
There was no reply, so Rupert walked in, and looked all around the room. The office was empty!
Rupert had an idea. He went back down the corridor and into the cloakroom.
"Kevin! Are you in here?" he asked.
There was no reply, but through the window Rupert saw a boy running out of the school gates.

Doctor Chimp was standing outside the cloakroom. He looked cross.
"I asked you to fetch Kevin from my office, Rupert," he began.
"He isn't there, Doctor Chimp!" cried Rupert. "Your office is empty, but I just saw a boy run out of the gates!"
Back in the classroom, the teacher told the class that Kevin had run away.
"He's new to Nutwood," said Bill Badger. "He might get lost."
"He must be found," said Doctor Chimp. "I will inform Constable Growler at once."
Rupert was worried.

"It's very cold outside. Shouldn't we look for Kevin, too?" he asked.

Doctor Chimp agreed.

"This wintry spell is no weather for runaways," he said. "We shall send out a search party!"

Outside, Constable Growler took charge of the hunt. He split the class into small groups. Some were sent to search the village, while others followed the road to Popton.

"Rupert, you take Bingo and Podgy," said the policeman. "See if there's any sign of Kevin down on the fields!"

Wrapped up warm in their winter coats, Rupert, Bingo and Podgy set off through the woods. When they reached the other side of the trees, the three friends looked down at the wide green fields.

"Look!" cried Bingo. "Over there!"
"That's not Kevin," laughed Podgy. "That's just a scarecrow!"
"Yes," said Rupert, "but why is it out today? It's far too early to grow corn!"
For a moment, they stared at the scarecrow. Suddenly, Podgy jumped. Something cold and wet had landed on his nose.
"Oh, no!" he shouted. "It's snowing!"
All around them, snowflakes began to swirl in the breeze.
"Kevin isn't here," said Rupert, "and we need somewhere to shelter."
The snow was falling faster and faster, covering the field like a carpet.
"There's a little hut over there," said Bingo, pointing across the field.
The three friends ran to the hut. The door was unlocked, and inside was warm and dry.
While the snow fell outside the hut, Rupert,

Bingo and Podgy chatted happily inside.
"I wonder if anyone has found Kevin yet," said Bingo.
"I expect so," replied Podgy. "He wouldn't go very far on a day like today!"
After a while, Rupert peered out of the door.
"It's stopped snowing," he said. "Let's go back to Nutwood before it starts again."
He led the way out of the hut and started to crunch through the crisp white snow which covered the field. Then he stopped, puzzled.
"The scarecrow's vanished!" he said, racing across the field to the place where it had been.
"There's no sign of it. But look!" Rupert exclaimed. "There's a set of footprints in the snow!"
Bingo pointed out to the others that scarecrows cannot walk.

"But this one did!" said Podgy. "I bet that if we followed the footprints, we would find the scare-crow."

Podgy and Bingo turned away, ready to track down the scarecrow, but Rupert stayed where he was. Something was puzzling him.

"These footprints don't lead away from the spot where the scarecrow was," he told his friends. "They lead right up to the spot — and then stop!"

Podgy tried his foot in the footprint. "You're right," he told Rupert. "That means that someone walked up to the scarecrow, and then simply vanished with it!"

"A scarecrow thief!" said Bingo. "With a friend in a helicopter to make his escape!"

"That's it!" cried Podgy. "Come on! Let's find Constable Growler and tell him!"

Bingo and Podgy set off again eagerly, but Rupert was still thinking.

"I'll catch you up," he called to his friends as they ran back towards Nutwood.

He was sure that no-one would try to fly a helicopter in such bad weather. Who would steal a scarecrow anyway? And why was the scarecrow out so early in the year? The mystery was just beginning, thought Rupert.

He decided to follow the footprints back to where they started.

Rupert tracked the stranger's path across the field. At the edge of the woods, he stopped,

surprised. There was another shed, like the one he and his friends had used to keep dry, and the footprints started from its door.

Rupert was sure that the answer to the mystery was inside the hut. Slowly, he opened the door. When he saw what was inside the shed, he nearly jumped out of his boots.

There was the scarecrow!

"Hello!" it said. "Who are you?"

"I'm Rupert," said the little bear. "You're Kevin, aren't you? What are you doing here?"

"I was sent to a new school today," said the little boy. "They all knew each other and I didn't know anybody, so I ran away and came to hide in this shed. These old clothes were lying here and — "

"You pretended to be a scarecrow!" cried Rupert. "Wait till I tell everyone how you tricked us with your disguise!"

Kevin grinned. He was proud of his plan.

"In fact, I've got a better idea," said Rupert.

"Come back to school with me and tell them yourself. They all want to meet you."

"Really?" asked Kevin.

"Really," said Rupert, and he led the way out of the hut into the crisp winter air.

"This way," said Rupert. "By the way, how did you get back here? The footprints all lead away from the hut."

Without a word, Kevin began to walk across the field, backwards.

With each step he left a neat footprint facing towards Rupert.

"I didn't think anyone would find me if I left a trail leading away from the hut," said Kevin. "But I'm glad you did!"

Rupert
and the Crock of Gold

It was a sunny Saturday morning in Nutwood. Rupert and his mother and father were eating their breakfast.

"It's a lovely day today, Rupert," said Mrs Bear. "Why don't you ask some of your friends to a picnic on the fields?"

"Thanks, Mummy," said Rupert. "I'll ask Bingo and Edward."

After breakfast, Rupert and his mother began to prepare the picnic. Suddenly, Rupert heard a clattering, pattering noise from the garden. He looked out of the kitchen window.

"Oh, no!" he cried in dismay. "It's pouring with rain!"

"It's only an April shower," his mother told him. "It won't last very long."

Sure enough, the shower passed quickly and the sun shone through the clouds once more.

Mrs Bear looked out of the window again.

"Just look at that!" she said.

In the sky was a perfect rainbow. The colours were so bright and clear that Rupert felt sure he could touch them.

"They say there's a crock of gold at the end of every rainbow," said his mother. "But no one can ever take any of it."

"Why can't they take the gold?" asked Rupert. "What will happen?"

"It's a mystery," replied Mrs Bear.

"If anyone ever comes too close to the crock of gold, the rainbow just vanishes!"

A good mystery, thought Rupert, is just what I need on a wet Saturday. He put on his coat and set off to meet his friends.

But when he turned the corner, he saw the rainbow again. It seemed to touch the ground just behind the tall pagoda where his friend the Chinese conjurer lived.

Rupert was determined to find the gold at the rainbow's end. When he came to the pagoda, Rupert began to run. I must hurry, he thought, before the rainbow vanishes. He rushed around the pagoda and raced to the spot where the rainbow touched the ground.

But the rainbow had disappeared.
Rupert stood by the pagoda, disappointed and out of breath.
"Training for school sports day, Rupert?"
Rupert turned round to see Tigerlily

skipping down the path.
"No, I, um, oh, dear," he panted.
"So where were you going in such a hurry?" asked Tigerlily.
"Well, here, I think," he replied. "But when I got here, it wasn't here, and now I don't know where to go."
"What wasn't here?" frowned Tigerlily.
"The rainbow," sighed Rupert. "I thought that if I ran really fast, I could catch the end of the rainbow and see the crock of gold. But now it's gone. It must be magic!"
"Well, if it is magic," said Tigerlily, "we'll find a spell in one of Daddy's books."
"Shouldn't we ask your father first?" asked Rupert.
"He's busy," said Tigerlily quickly. "We'd better not disturb him."

Inside the pagoda, Tigerlily led Rupert to her father's library. She took a very old, very heavy book down from the shelf and laid it on her father's reading desk.

"Let's see," she said. "Clouds, gales, monsoons, rain—rainbows!"

Rupert leaned across to see what the book said. Behind him, a secret door opened.

"Helping Rupert with his homework, Tigerlily?" asked the Chinese conjurer.

Rupert and Tigerlily jumped up.

"No, no, just reading," said Tigerlily.

"Just reading my book of spells," said her father, looking very stern. "Why were you reading my book?"

Rupert took a deep breath, and told the

conjurer about the rainbow.

"Do you really want to see the gold?" asked Tigerlily's father.

"Yes," answered Rupert.

"I do have a spell which will take you to the end of the rainbow," said the conjurer.

Tigerlily tugged at her father's sleeve.

"Oh Daddy," she cried. "Let me go too!"
"Very well, Tigerlily," said the Chinese conjurer. "But you must both promise me that you will not touch the gold."
"We promise," they said.
"Now, come out to the garden," said the conjurer.
Rupert and Tigerlily followed him outside. In the garden, the conjurer uttered his magic spell. Rupert looked up at the grey sky. Slowly, it began to glow with bright, clear colours.
"The rainbow!" he cried.
"Hold hands, please," said the conjurer. "Walk straight ahead."
In front of them was a damp, foggy cloud. Together, Rupert and Tigerlily walked slowly into it.
"Where are we?" asked Tigerlily.
Rupert looked down. A fine mist swirled around his feet, then rose like a marvellous coloured fountain and curved away over their heads.
"We're at the end of the rainbow!" he gasped. "Look! Down there!"
At the very foot of the arch was a pot, just like the ones in his mother's larder. It was filled to the brim with the purest, most precious gold.
"Look at that!" cried Rupert. "Just wait till I tell Bingo and Edward!"
Tigerlily bent over the crock.
"They'll never believe you," she said.
"I wouldn't make up a story like this," replied Rupert. "They know I wouldn't. Come on, Tigerlily, I think it's time we went back to Nutwood."

"All right," said Tigerlily, reluctantly. "Let's just have one more look at the rainbow first."

Rupert craned his neck to look up at the beautiful arch over their heads. Tigerlily watched him until she was sure he was looking the other way. Then she reached into the pot of gold.

"Ready?" asked Rupert. "Hold my hand."

They walked together back through the cloud again. When the mist cleared, Rupert looked around.

"That's funny," he said. "We haven't arrived in your father's garden. We're on Nutwood Common! Look! There's Bingo, and Edward!"

"Rupert! Tigerlily!" cried Bingo. "Where have you been?"

"I was just on my way to meet you," Rupert told his friends.

"Tigerlily and I have had a wonderful adventure. We went to the end of the rainbow. We've seen the crock of gold!"

Before Bingo or Edward could say a word, Tigerlily rushed forward.

"I can prove it!" she said.

She reached inside her robe and pulled out something small and yellow. She held it under Bingo's nose.

"Look!" she said. "Real gold, from the rainbow's end!"

Bingo and Edward looked at Tigerlily's gold coin.

Suddenly, Rupert had a horrible, sinking feeling. His friends were laughing!

"Very good, Tigerlily!" chuckled Edward.

"It looks just like gold!" giggled Bingo.

"You must think we're April fools!" laughed Edward.

Tigerlily looked at her piece of gold, and saw that it wasn't gold at all. It was a yellow pebble, as dull as any on the beach.

Rupert turned away. Standing quietly to one side, Tigerlily's father, the Chinese conjurer, was looking sterner than ever.

"I don't understand," said Rupert. "I saw real gold at the rainbow's end!"

"Your friends believed you until they saw Tigerlily's pebble," replied the conjurer. "Now they think it's just a joke."

"But it isn't!" cried Rupert.

"Tigerlily!" said the Chinese conjurer. "What did you promise?"

"I promised not to touch the gold," said his daughter, looking very ashamed.

"Yes, you did," said the conjurer. "Bingo! Edward! Do you know what there is at the rainbow's end?"

"A crock of gold!" they cried.

"You see?" asked the conjurer. "No need to prove it."

"I'm sorry, Daddy," said Tigerlily.

"So you should be, Tigerlily," replied her father. "For there is magic, too, at the rainbow's end."

"You were really there!" said Bingo.

"Yes, we really were," said Rupert. "Mind you, I prefer Nutwood."

"Why?" asked Edward, looking puzzled.

"I'd choose my friends over a crock of gold any day," he said, as it began to rain again.

Rupert
and the Curious Car

"Eggs, tomatoes, carrots — now, what else do I need?" Mrs Bear was writing her shopping list. "Uncle Bruno's coming, so I had better buy plenty."

"Shall I do the shopping for you?" asked Rupert.

Mrs Bear was very pleased that Rupert was so thoughtful.

"I think that's everything," she said, picking up the list. "No, not quite!" and she added something at the end.

"I shan't be long," said Rupert, putting the shopping list in his trouser pocket.

Rupert set off for Mrs Fox's General Store in Nutwood. As he walked down the path, he saw someone strolling along in front of him.

Rupert quickly caught him up.

"Hello, Doctor Lion," he said.

The doctor did not reply, but carried on walking, looking very serious.

"Are you feeling all right?" asked Rupert.

Doctor Lion looked at the little bear.

"I'm sorry, Rupert. I was miles away," he said. "Something very odd happened last night when I was visiting one of my patients. I can't understand it!"

"What happened?" asked Rupert.

"Edward Trunk had a tummy upset," said Doctor Lion, "so I jumped in the car and rushed round to see him. I was in such a hurry that I left the keys in the car."

"Oh, no," gasped Rupert. "Someone stole your car!"

"No, Rupert," replied Doctor Lion. "No one stole the car."

"Then what's wrong?" asked Rupert.
"When I went back, the car was locked — and my keys were still inside it!"
"Oh, dear," said Rupert. "How are you going to get in?"
"I'm on my way to the locksmith now," said the doctor. "He'll help. I don't know how the door locked itself. It's a mystery!"
At the corner, Rupert said goodbye to Doctor Lion and carried on towards the general store. He decided to call in on Mrs Trunk on the way to find out how his friend was feeling.
It was a fine morning and the air was full of birdsong, but as Rupert came closer to the Trunks' house, he noticed another sound: a horrible banging and thumping.
Across the road was Doctor Lion's car, still parked where he had left it the night before. Rupert went to have a look at it.

The banging seemed to come from inside the car. He peered through the window — and had quite a shock.
Glaring out at him was an angry face.
"You!" came a fierce little voice. "I might have known it was you! Let me out!"

"Raggety!" cried Rupert. "What are you doing in Doctor Lion's car?"

"Let me out first," said Raggety angrily. "Then you can tell me why you shut me in this stupid box!"

"But I didn't!" cried Rupert.

Raggety took no notice of Rupert. He just kept on banging and screaming, "Let me out!" at the top of his shrill voice.

"Listen, Raggety," said Rupert. "If you stop banging and shouting, I'll help you to get out."

"Hurry up," said Raggety crossly.

Rupert told Raggety how to unlock the car door from the inside.

"A likely story," said Raggety, as he reached for the door handle.

The old car door creaked open and Raggety climbed out.

He yawned, stretched and then turned to Rupert with a frown.

"So I could have escaped from that nasty trap last night, could I?" he asked.

"It's not a trap," said Rupert. "It's Doctor Lion's car. Why were you in it, anyway?"

"It was cold last night," complained Raggety.

"I climbed in to warm myself up and shut the door to keep out the draughts."

"You must have locked the door by mistake," said Rupert. "But didn't you hear Doctor Lion trying to open the door?"

"It was so lovely and snug in there that I fell asleep. The next thing I heard was the dawn chorus," said Raggety. "I've been trapped in that horrible thing for ages! I don't want to see another car ever again!"

Rupert watched as Raggety stomped off across Nutwood Common.

Rupert looked inside the car again, and spotted the doctor's keys. He picked them up,

shut the door and locked it. Then he carefully crossed the road and ran towards the shops. If he was quick, he could catch Doctor Lion at the locksmith's.

Rupert dashed into the locksmith's shop and handed the doctor his keys. He didn't notice a small piece of paper falling out of his pocket onto the locksmith's floor.

"Thank you, Rupert," said Doctor Lion. "You're just in time! But how did you get my keys out of the car?"

Rupert told him all about Raggety's night in the cosy car.

"I was only passing your car because I wanted to see how Edward was feeling," he explained.

"Edward's fine now," said Doctor Lion.

"I'm glad he's better," said Rupert. Then he remembered why he had walked into Nutwood. "Oh, no!" he cried. "I haven't done the shopping!"

After Rupert had left the shop, the locksmith pointed to something on the floor. "Look! What's that?"

Doctor Lion picked up the piece of paper and read it carefully.

"Hey, Rupert!"

Rupert was on his way to Mrs Fox's shop when he heard someone calling him.

"Hello, Bill! Hello, Algy!" He turned and greeted his friends.

"We're going round to see how Edward's feeling," said Bill. "His mother had to call the

doctor last night."

"I know," said Rupert. "You'll never guess what happened to Doctor Lion's car while he was in the Trunks' house."

Bill and Algy listened intently while Rupert told them the whole story. None of them noticed Doctor Lion walk quietly by on the other side of the road.

"So you didn't go to see Edward after all," said Algy.

"Why don't you come with us now?" asked Bill.

"I'm afraid I'll have to see him later," replied Rupert. "I'm just going for some shopping for my mother."

Rupert waved goodbye to his friends and walked down the street and into the general store.

"Good morning, Rupert," said Mrs Fox. "What can I do for you today?"

"Hello, Mrs Fox. My mother needs some extra provisions," said Rupert. "She's given me a shopping list."

Rupert put his hand in his pocket and pulled out — nothing! He tried the other pocket. It was empty, too. He had lost the shopping list!

Mrs Fox looked concerned. "Have you lost something, Rupert?" she asked.

Before Rupert could reply, Mrs Fox put a bag full of groceries on the counter.

"It's all right," she said. "Doctor Lion found the list on the locksmith's floor and brought it straight round to me. I've already packed your shopping for you!"

Rupert thanked Mrs Fox and walked home as quickly as he could.

Mrs Bear was in the kitchen.

"Let's see what you've brought for me," she said, unpacking the shopping bag.

"Eggs, tomatoes, carrots — what's this?"

Mrs Bear took out a packet of biscuits and handed them to Rupert.

"They're my favourites!" said Rupert.

"I know," said Mrs Bear. "Thank you for doing the shopping, Rupert. And you were so quick, too!"

Rupert
and the Ghost Train

One afternoon, Rupert Bear, Bill Badger and Algy Pug went for a long walk.

"Look at Algy," laughed Bill, "a little stroll and he's worn out!"

"I am not tired," said Algy. "I'll even race you both home!"

Before his friends could answer, he ran off down the lane.

"Come on, Rupert!" called Bill. "We'll show him!"

Algy heard their footsteps coming closer and closer. They were going to catch him!

"Whoa, there. Slow down!"

Algy skidded to a halt.

"Always in a hurry, that's the trouble with you youngsters." Gaffer Jarge waved his walking stick angrily.

"Let's just stop for a minute," panted Algy. He was quite out of breath.

"Coming down that hill like an express train, you were," grumbled Gaffer Jarge.

"Sorry," said Rupert. "Don't you like trains, then?"

"Never been on one, and I hope I never do," replied the Gaffer. "Seen plenty, mind you. There's one on its way right now!"

"I can't hear anything," said Bill.

"Look," replied Gaffer Jarge, pointing across the fields.

In the distance, a row of little steam clouds rose above the railway line. Gaffer Jarge pulled out his old watch.

"Fast train to the south coast," he said. "Two minutes late!"

"That reminds me," said Rupert. "Last night, I heard a train go by in the middle of the night."

"So did I," said Algy, "and the night before, too. I've never noticed it before."

"There are no trains in the middle of the night," said Gaffer Jarge. "Never have been, and I hope there never will."

"Well, I heard it!" said Bill. "Perhaps it's a ghost train!"

Rupert had an idea.

"If we all go to the station tonight, we can watch out for the mystery train," he said. "You youngsters can go," said Gaffer Jarge. "I shall be tucked up snug in my bed!"

Rupert, Bill and Algy asked their parents for permission to watch for the mysterious train. That night they waited at Rupert's house until it was time to go to the station. It was very late when Mrs Bear waved goodbye to Rupert and his friends.

"Be very careful," she told them, "and whatever you do, make sure you don't go near the railway line."

Before they had reached the garden gate, Mrs Bear ran after them.

"Bill! Wait!" she cried. "You've forgotten your scarf!"

Bill raced back to the cottage and put on his warm, woollen scarf.

Rupert, Bill and Algy walked down the lane towards the station.

"We'll sit in the waiting room until we hear the train," whispered Rupert.

He walked up to the station door and turned the handle, but it was locked. Algy pressed his nose to the window.

"There's nobody there," he said, "and no more trains due until the morning!"

"Let's wait a while," said Rupert.

The three friends stood outside the station.

It was very dark, and there wasn't a sound to be heard until clunk! A strange noise came from out of the darkness.

"What was that?" asked Bill nervously.

Algy pointed towards the far end of the station platform.

"It was the signal changing," he said. "The train must be coming from Popton!"

Rupert shone his torch on the path beside the station wall.

"Look, this path runs beside the railway line all the way to Popton," he said. "Let's follow it. If we stay on this side of the fence, we'll be quite safe."

The path took Algy, Bill and Rupert through the woods. It was very dark, and the trees creaked and groaned in the breeze.

"Oh, dear," said Bill. "I hope our mystery train isn't a ghost train!"

Now the huffing and puffing of the train could be heard in the distance. Rupert leaned over the fence to look down the line. Quickly, he turned back to his friends. Something was wrong!

"There's a fallen tree on the line!" he cried. "We mustn't let the train hit it!"

"What can we do?" asked Bill. "It's not safe to go near the track!"

Rupert knew a way.

"Bill, you and Algy must run as fast as you can to that clearing in the woods. Then..."

His friends listened carefully, then set off along the path. As they ran away, Rupert could hear the train rattling nearer and nearer to the fallen tree. Then he heard a rustling in the woods.

"What's all this fuss?" asked a cross little voice. "Why, it's Rupert!"

Suddenly, tiny doors began to open in some nearby tree trunks. The noise had woken the Imps of Spring!

"Look!" said Rupert, pointing to the railway line. "There's a tree on the line, and a train is on its way!"

"Then we must move that tree at once!" ordered a stern voice. It was the King of the Imps.

"Algy and Bill are waiting for the train," Rupert told him. "I have a plan to stop it."

"A plan, eh?" said the King.

"Yes, and if it works, the train will stop before it reaches the tree," said Rupert.

From further down the line came a shrill whistle. Then Rupert and the King heard a screech of brakes as the heavy engine shuddered to a halt near where Bill and Algy stood.

"Forward, Imps! Forward to the fallen tree!" cried the King, and dozens of tiny men ran under the fence and onto the track.

"One, two, three — lift!" the King ordered.

The tree was heavy, and the Imps groaned under its weight, but slowly it began to move. Inch by inch, they carried it to the side of the track, where it was safely out of the train's way. Then the little men gave a loud cheer.

"What was that?" asked a strange voice.

Rupert turned round. The engine driver was marching towards him.

"My friends — " said Rupert, pointing to the far side of the track.

There was no-one to be seen, although something that might have been a tiny pair of eyes glinted out of the hedgerow.

Rupert smiled to himself.

"My friends moved that tree off the line for you," he explained.

The driver was very puzzled.

"They must be very strong," he said.

"It's lucky you were here to warn me about the fallen tree. And that plan of yours was very clever!"

"See how well it works!" said Bill. He took off his scarf and stretched it over the end of his torch so that a red light shone brightly.

"That's a stop signal if ever I saw one!" laughed the driver.

"If you're not a ghost train," said Rupert, "then why are you out so late at night?"

"Come back to the wagons and see for yourselves," replied the driver.

Rupert, Bill and Algy followed the driver down the path to the first of the trucks.

"Special service," said the driver. "It's Mother's Day tomorrow, and the markets need all the flowers they can get."

He opened the wagon door.

"Here you are," he said, "three bunches of fresh flowers. Wish your mothers each a happy Mother's Day from me!" the driver added.

"Thank you," replied the three friends.

Rupert, Bill and Algy had begun to walk back to Nutwood when the engine driver called them back.

"Don't forget your scarf, Bill!" he laughed. "You never know when you might need it!"

Rupert
and the Rhyming Riddle

It was a fine summer's evening. Rupert Bear and Bill Badger had spent their first afternoon on holiday building a sandcastle. Now it was high tide and the waves were lapping at the battlements. Bill picked up a flat, smooth pebble from the shore.

"Watch this," he said.

Bill threw the pebble sideways so that it skimmed across the water, bouncing before it sank below the surface.

"I say, you stop that!"

Rupert turned round to see a smartly dressed man standing behind him.

"That's my yacht over there — the Lucky Lil — and I don't want you throwing stones at her!" said the man.

"He wasn't throwing stones at your yacht," Rupert protested.

"Just go away — now!" the man ordered.

Sadly, Rupert and Bill scrambled up to the path above the beach, then stopped to look back at the Lucky Lil. Captain Binnacle came down the path from his house and joined them. He had seen the stranger talking to Rupert and Bill.

"I wish I had a yacht like that," said Bill.

"Aye, shipmates, she's a fine vessel," said Captain Binnacle. "Can't say I like her captain much, though."

Rupert told Captain Binnacle how nasty the stranger had been to Bill.

"Never mind," he said. "Rosie, my niece, will be here tomorrow. Why don't I ask her to meet you by those rocks on the beach?"

Next day, Bill and Rupert went to meet the Captain's niece. They clambered over the rocks onto the headland and looked all around, but Rosie was nowhere to be seen.

"Where can she be?" asked Bill.

"Rupert! Bill!"

They looked round again, but could still see no one.

"Over here!" cried Rosie.

There she was, peeping out of a hole in the side of the headland! Rupert and Bill scrambled up to join her.

"It's a cave!" said Rupert.

"Yes," said Rosie, "and there's something in here. Come and look!"

Inside the cave, they found a battered old sea chest. It was padlocked, and there was a crumpled label tied to the handle. In the dim light of the cave, Rupert could just read the writing.

Rosie and Bill listened as Rupert read out the message that was on the label.

"The secret of this treasure chest
Will be yours if you find the key.
So look down below the crow's nest
On the ship that never goes to sea!"

"It's a treasure chest!" gasped Bill. "We must find that key!"

"First, we must solve the rhyming riddle," said Rupert. "The message says the key is hidden below the crow's nest on a ship that never goes to sea. I know a crow's nest is the lookout platform on a ship."

Rosie pointed to the boats in the harbour.

"Perhaps it means a ship that never leaves its moorings," she said. "Like a houseboat. Let's go and look!"
Rosie scrambled eagerly over the rocks and ran down the path towards the harbour. She ran up to the Harbour Master, who was outside his hut polishing his brass bell.
"You know all the boats in Rocky Bay, don't you?" she asked.

"No one drops anchor without my say-so," agreed the Harbour Master.
"And," Rosie carried on quickly, "are there any boats which never go to sea?"
"Why yes," he replied. "Old Smuggler Sam hasn't taken the Sea Breeze out in years."
Bill, Rosie and Rupert looked at each other. They couldn't believe their luck.
"Smuggler Sam!" they cried.
"Of course, he's not a real smuggler,"

said the Harbour Master. "He just likes the name."
But Rupert and his friends didn't hear the Harbour Master. They were already searching for the Sea Breeze. A little further down the quay, they spotted a wizened man aboard a battered old boat.

"Excuse me," began Rupert. "Could we have a look at your crow's nest, please?"
"Crow's nest?" Smuggler Sam laughed. "This boat's too small for a crow's nest! There's barely room for a seagull to perch up that mast!"
Bill looked very disappointed.
"No crow's nest means no key," he said sadly.

"And no key means — "

"No treasure!" said Rupert and Rosie together.

Rupert looked along the row of boats moored in the little bay. None of them had a crow's nest.

"We'll never find the key now," said Bill.

"Let's go back and ask my uncle to help us," said Rosie. "I'm sure he'll know the answer to the riddle."

Rupert, Bill and Rosie walked up the path towards Captain Binnacle's cabin.

Bill pointed to a hotel on the seafront.

"Look! There's the Ship Inn. That's where we're staying," he told Rosie.

Rupert stopped walking.

"The Ship Inn!" he cried. "Now, that's a ship that never goes to sea!"

"Come on, you two!" said Rosie, running down the path. "We'll find the key there. I'm sure we will!"

The three friends ran to the Ship Inn.

"Where's the crow's nest?" asked Bill, when they had arrived.

"Follow me," said Rupert.

He led them round to the hotel garden, and pointed up at the old oak tree. High in its branches was a mass of twigs.

"There's the crow's nest!" he said. "The key must be somewhere below it."

Bill rushed forward and reached into a hollow in the side of the tree trunk.

"Is there anything there?" asked Rosie.

The smile on Bill's face grew wider and wider as he pulled out his hand.

"Yes!" he said. "It's a key!"

On the way back to the cave, Bill didn't stop talking.

"What do you think is in that chest?" he asked. "It could be gold! There might be jewels in there. It's bound to be treasure, isn't it?"

At last they reached the cave.

"Try the key in the lock," said Rupert.

Bill turned the key, and with a click the padlock opened. He lifted the lid of the dusty old chest and looked inside. There was something there!

"The riddle says that if you find the key, you can have the treasure," Rupert said. "You found the key, Bill."

"I think we should share the treasure," said Bill firmly.

Bill reached into the chest and carefully lifted out a hand-carved model yacht.

"Let's take it outside," he said.

There, in the warm summer sunshine, Rupert, Bill and Rosie admired the beautiful model boat. Everything about it was perfect — the sails, the rigging, even the name painted on the side.

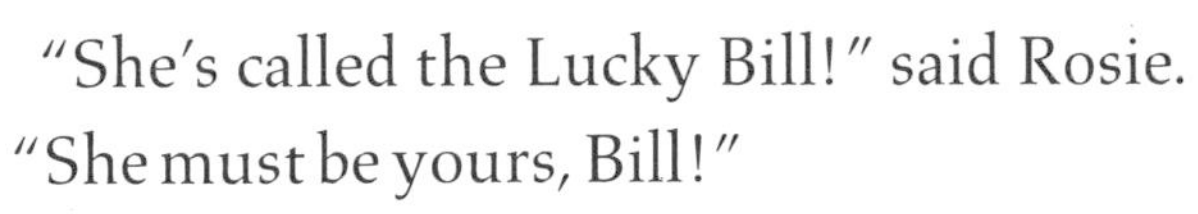

"She's called the Lucky Bill!" said Rosie. "She must be yours, Bill!"

Bill ran down to the water's edge and launched his yacht into the gently bobbing sea.

Rupert and Rosie followed him.

"Rosie," said Rupert, "I'm very glad you discovered that cave."

"Well, my uncle told me where to find it," replied Rosie.

Captain Binnacle was sitting outside his cabin, carving a piece of wood. He watched Rupert, Bill and Rosie playing with the yacht, and smiled to himself.